How and Why Science

Science in the Air

How and Why Science

Science in the Air

World Book, Inc.
Chicago London Sydney Toronto

Acknowledgments

The publisher of Childcraft gratefully acknowledge the courtesy of illustrator John Sandford and the following photographers, agencies, and organizations for the illustrations in this volume. Credits should be read from left to right, top to bottom, on their respective pages. All illustrations are the exclusive property of the publisher of Childcraft unless names are marked with an asterisk (*).

8-9 NASA/Science Source from Photo Researchers*
16-17 Glenn M. Oliver, Visuals Unlimited*; A. D. Copley, Visuals Unlimited*
20-21 National Weather Service*
24-25 A & J Verlaik, The Stock Market*
26-27 Lancing College Archives*
28-29 Richard B. Alley, Penn State University*; Ken Abbott, Colorado University, Boulder*

World Book, Inc.
525 West Monroe
Chicago, IL 60661

Editors: Sharon Nowakowski, Melissa Tucker
Art Director: Wilma Stevens
Illustrator: John Sandford
Cover design: Susan Newman
Cover Illustrator: Eileen Mueller Neill

Library of Congress Cataloging-in-Publication Data

Science in the air.
p. cm. -- (How and why science)
Includes index.
Summary: Describes various weather phenomena that cause changes in the atmosphere and explains how to read clues to the weather in the air around us.
ISBN 0-7166-7111-5 (pbk.)
1. Weather--Juvenile literature. 2. Meteorology--Juvenile literature. 3. Air--Juvenile literature. 4. Air--Experiments--Juvenile literature. [1. Weather. 2. Air.] I. World Book, Inc. II. Series.
QC981.3.S35 1998
551.5--dc21 98-15675

For information on other World Book products, call 1-800-255-1750, x2238, or visit us at our Web site at http://www.worldbook.com

Printed in Singapore

2 3 4 5 6 7 8 9 02 01 00 99

Introduction

You can't see it, smell it, or taste it, but life on this planet would be impossible without it. One way that you can experience what air does is to notice the weather. Look out the window. Do you see any signs of air's activities? Are branches or leaves blowing in the breeze? Will today be a good day for a picnic, or are the conditions telling you a storm is on the way?

Science helps people answer questions such as, "Is air heavier on some days than others? What is a storm front? What was the weather like millions of years ago?" **Science in the Air** shows you new ways to look at air—even though you can't see it!

In this book, all kinds of scientists explain how they study the world. They'll show you how to read clues in the air. Don't worry about not understanding unfamiliar words, they are defined in the margins. Science folklore adds to the fun. The **Aha!** feature highlights surprising science facts. When you are ready to try your skills, check out the **In Your Lab** sections.

Science is not just for professional meteorologists or climatologists. Science helps all of us understand the world around us, even those things we can't see.

How Thin Is Thin Air?

AHA!

Earth's atmosphere is about 600 miles (966 km) thick and weighs an astonishing 5 3/4 quadrillion tons (5 1/4 quadrillion metric tons). That's heavy!

Do you think air is a lightweight subject? Think again. You can study air all your life and still be amazed by it. In this book, you'll learn a lot about air, including why it's important to know so much about it.

Air is invisible, but that doesn't mean there is nothing to it. Air is a mixture of gases that swirls around our planet. Wave your hand through the air. Did you feel anything? You just waved your hand through gases, mostly nitrogen and a lot of oxygen. Air also has *water vapor* (water in the form of a gas), carbon dioxide, and other gases. These invisible gases weigh more than you might expect. They are like blankets that circle the earth, and gravity pulls on them. The weight of these blankets as they press down on the earth is called air pressure or *atmospheric pressure* (AT muh SFIR ihk PREHSH uhr).

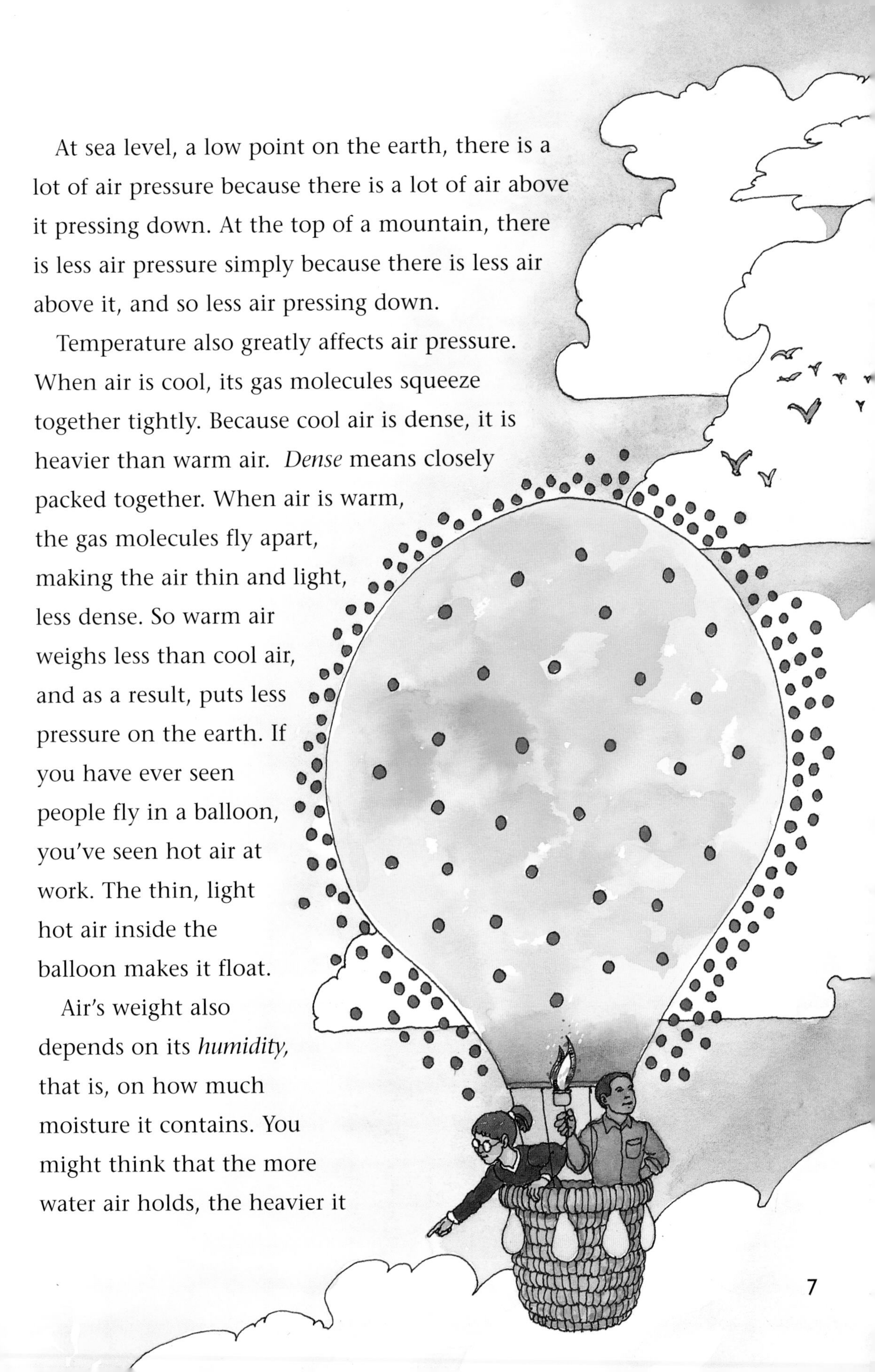

At sea level, a low point on the earth, there is a lot of air pressure because there is a lot of air above it pressing down. At the top of a mountain, there is less air pressure simply because there is less air above it, and so less air pressing down.

Temperature also greatly affects air pressure. When air is cool, its gas molecules squeeze together tightly. Because cool air is dense, it is heavier than warm air. *Dense* means closely packed together. When air is warm, the gas molecules fly apart, making the air thin and light, less dense. So warm air weighs less than cool air, and as a result, puts less pressure on the earth. If you have ever seen people fly in a balloon, you've seen hot air at work. The thin, light hot air inside the balloon makes it float.

Air's weight also depends on its *humidity,* that is, on how much moisture it contains. You might think that the more water air holds, the heavier it would be. But the opposite is true. Air with a lot of moisture in it is less dense. Something that is less dense is packed together less closely. So air that is less dense is also less heavy. This means that moist air is lighter than dry air. The heaviest air is cool and dry. The lightest air is warm and moist.

Earth is covered with a constantly changing pattern of high-pressure areas and low-pressure areas. These are known as *pressure systems,* and they are responsible for our weather.

When the air pressure is low in a certain area, meteorologists call that area a "low." You've probably seen *LOW* or *L* on weather maps. The air around a low is usually warm and moist, so clouds and rain are likely.

An area where the air pressure is high, or heavy, is called a "high." Have you seen *HIGH* or *H* on weather maps? The air around a high is usually dry and often cool, so sunny skies and clear weather are in the forecast.

AHA!

The higher you go in the atmosphere, the less oxygen your body takes in with each breath. Most people feel dizzy at 10,000 feet (3,050 m) above sea level. Mountain climbers may camp for a few nights at one altitude to let their bodies adapt.

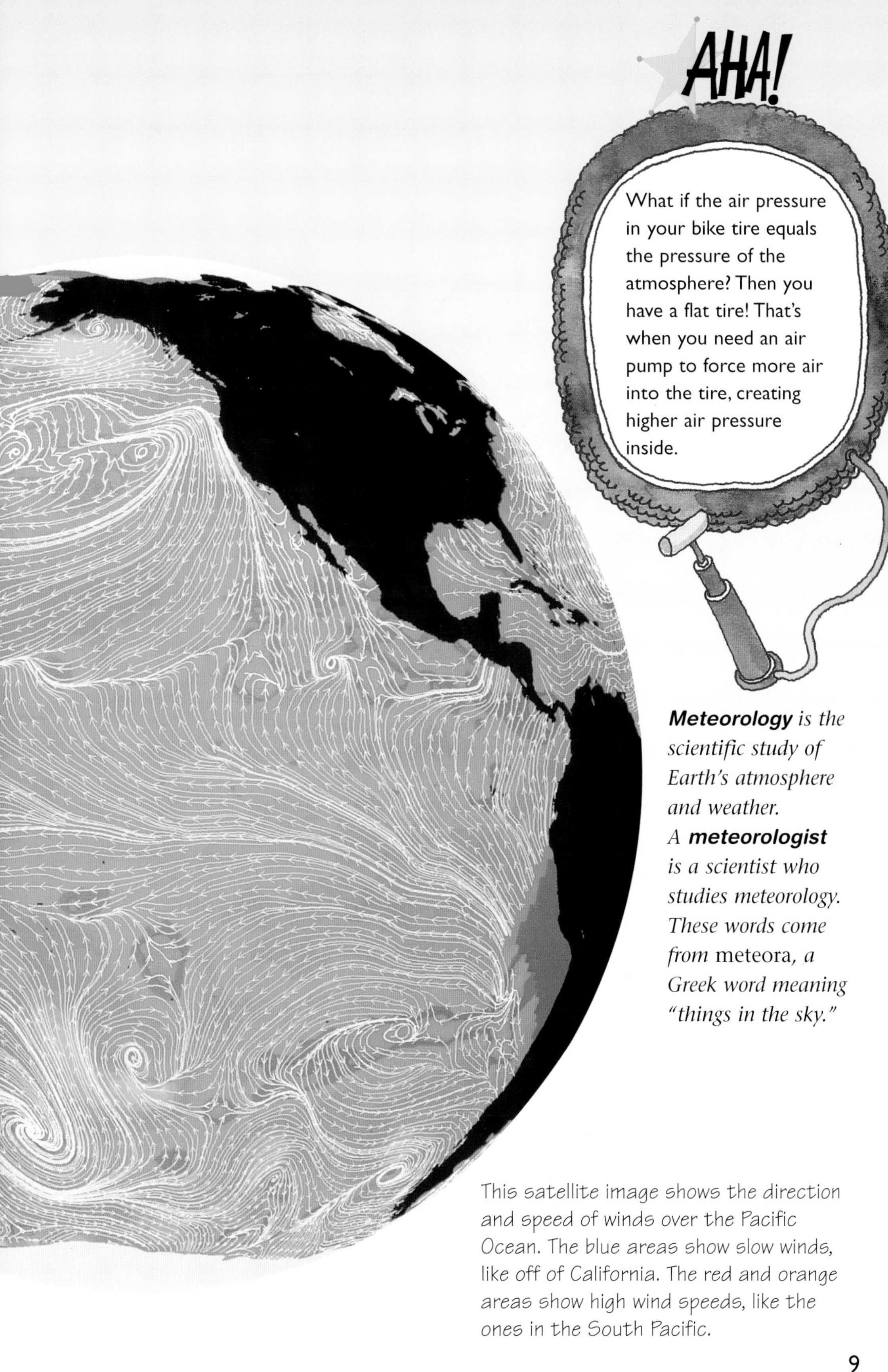

***Meteorology** is the scientific study of Earth's atmosphere and weather. A **meteorologist** is a scientist who studies meteorology. These words come from* meteora, *a Greek word meaning "things in the sky."*

This satellite image shows the direction and speed of winds over the Pacific Ocean. The blue areas show slow winds, like off of California. The red and orange areas show high wind speeds, like the ones in the South Pacific.

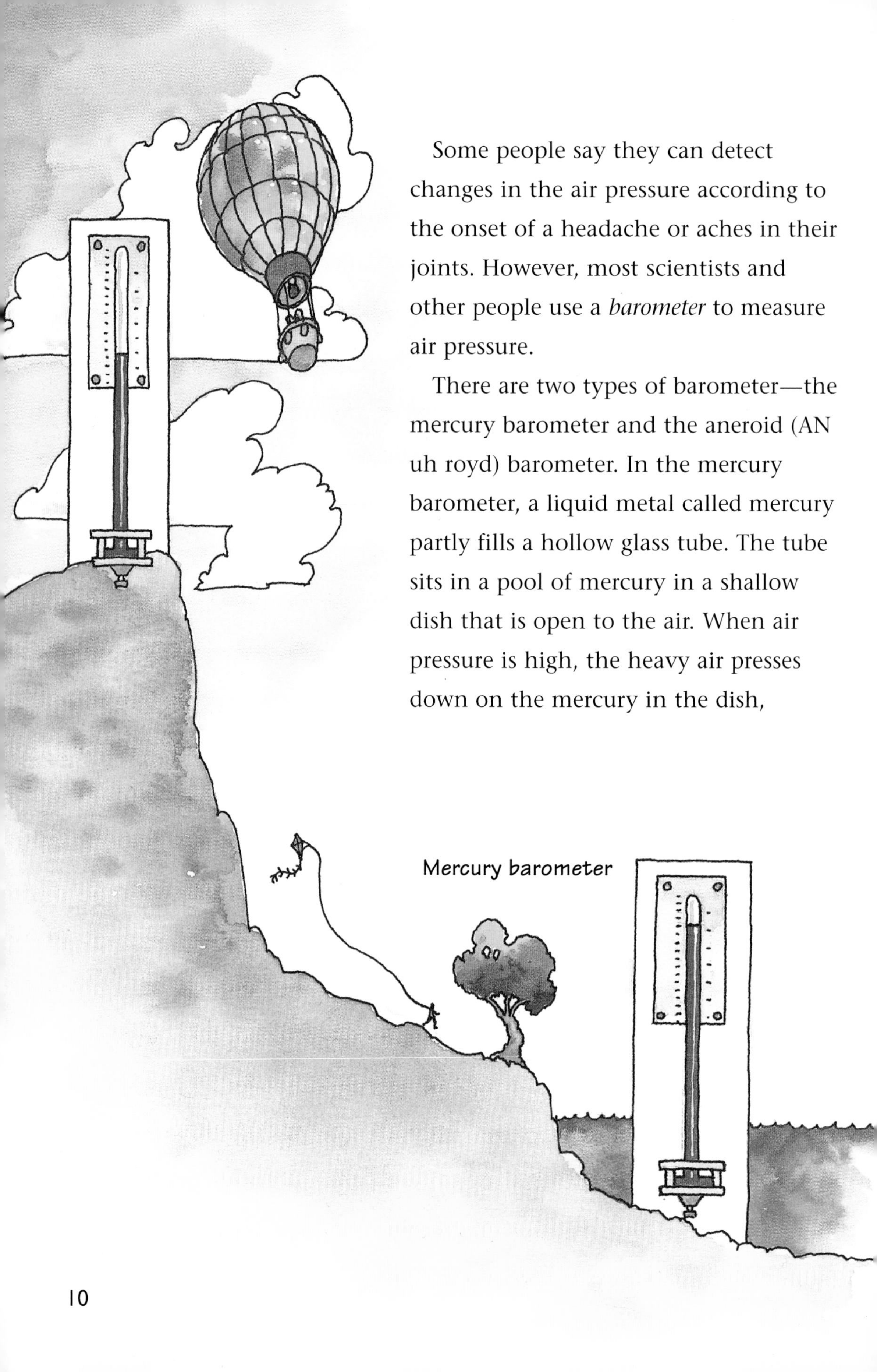

Some people say they can detect changes in the air pressure according to the onset of a headache or aches in their joints. However, most scientists and other people use a *barometer* to measure air pressure.

There are two types of barometer—the mercury barometer and the aneroid (AN uh royd) barometer. In the mercury barometer, a liquid metal called mercury partly fills a hollow glass tube. The tube sits in a pool of mercury in a shallow dish that is open to the air. When air pressure is high, the heavy air presses down on the mercury in the dish,

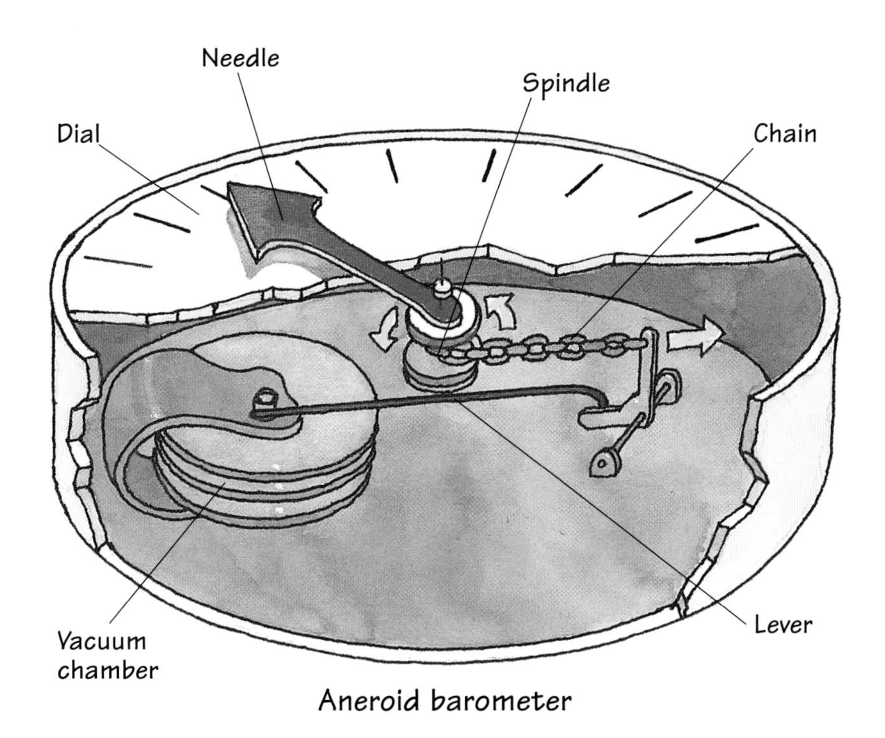

Aneroid barometer

forcing the mercury up the tube. When air pressure is low, the mercury in the tube drops and runs back into the dish.

The *aneroid barometer* contains a vacuum chamber—a metal container with no air inside. A drop in air pressure makes the chamber *expand* (get bigger) as the walls of the chamber move farther apart. A rise makes them *contract* (get smaller) as the walls are pushed closer together. The chamber is connected to a needle that moves around a dial, which we can read.

A high reading on a barometer indicates good weather. A low reading means that a storm may be on the way.

Today the barometer is staying nice and high. Looks like a great day for a picnic!

When you are standing up, the weight of about 2,000 pounds (907 kg) of air is pressing down on you! When you lie down, that weight is even greater. Luckily, you are supported by air pressure on all sides. Otherwise, you'd really feel a weight on your shoulders!

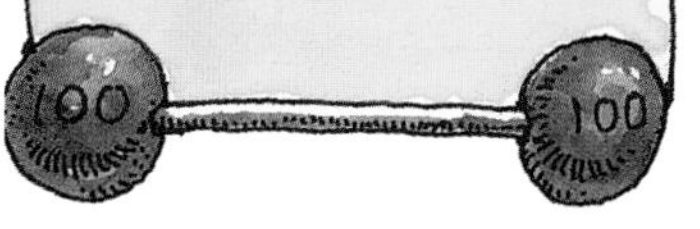

Make and Use a Barometer

Hmmmm . . . I wonder . . .
The weight of the air pressing down on Earth is always changing.
But how can I measure it?
How much does altitude affect air pressure?

GATHER TOOLS

- rubber balloon
- 2 identical glass jars
- rubber bands
- a paper soda straw
- glue
- a flat wooden toothpick
- a pencil
- scissors
- a craft stick

Set up and give it a try

1 Cut off the narrow end of a balloon—the end with the blow-hole—and throw it away. Save the rest of the balloon. Stretch the balloon piece tightly over the mouth of a jar. Fasten it tightly with a rubber band.

2 Flatten the straw. Cut one end into a pointed tip. Glue the other end to the balloon piece at the center.

3 Glue the toothpick to the balloon right at the top edge of the jar so that the straw rests on the wood. The straw is your barometer's "needle."

4 Using rubber bands, attach the craft stick to the outside of the other jar so that it sticks about 1 inch (2.5 cm) above the top edge of the jar.

Set up a control

Use a barometer from the store as a control. Or, watch TV weather reports and record the barometric pressure for your area.

5 Place the jars close together so that the sharp end of the "needle" points to the craft stick on the second jar. To avoid getting false readings, make sure your barometer is away from heat, air conditioning, and open windows.

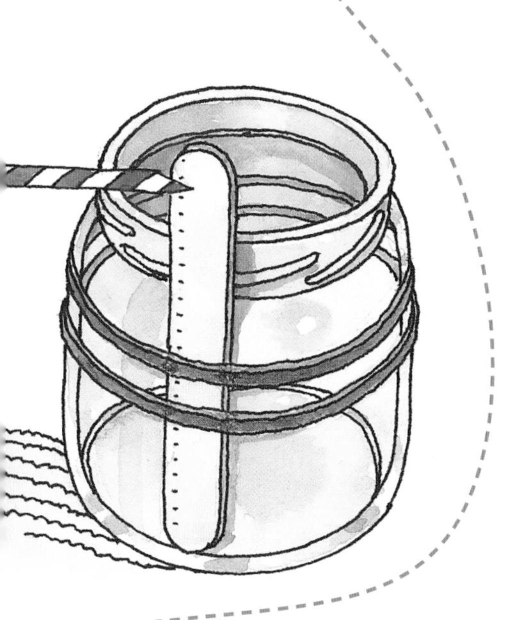

6 Check your barometer every day at the same time. Mark the spot on the stick where the needle points, and write the date beside it.

Try it again and again

- Take readings on the same day from high and low places, such as a hilltop or valley.
- Take readings for several weeks or for several days during different seasons.

Now, write it down

After a week, compare your barometric records with the ones from your control. Did your readings change when they did? Why do you think your readings match or don't match?

Compare your notes with the ones on page 32.

The *Front* of a Storm

Hi! I'm weather forecaster Rayne Gauge (GAYJ). It's my job to figure out what the weather will do next. To do so, I keep a close eye on air masses. Among other things, they help me tell you where a bad storm is lurking, and if today is a good day for a picnic.

You see, the air is not the same wherever you go. The world is covered by enormous clumps of air called *air masses*. An air mass forms over an area in which the temperature is fairly constant. The mass can cover hundreds of square miles and can be wet or dry, cold or hot, cool or warm. Dry, cold air masses develop over the dry, frigid poles. Wet, hot air masses develop over tropical oceans. Dry, hot air masses form over deserts.

Earth's rotation naturally causes air masses to move from one area to another.

Earth's rotation naturally causes air masses to move from one area to another. And as you already know, air masses take on the temperature of the area over which they move. However, they do so very slowly because of their great size. So before an area can greatly change an air mass, the air mass affects the area's weather.

Let me explain. When a cold air mass and a warm air mass meet, you have a zone that is called a *front*. Most changes in weather occur along fronts.

AHA!

A front may be the reason that you are wearing a bathing suit while someone a few hundred miles away needs a parka. A cold front often divides sharply different air masses. Sometimes the temperature difference can be 50 °F (28 °C) or more.

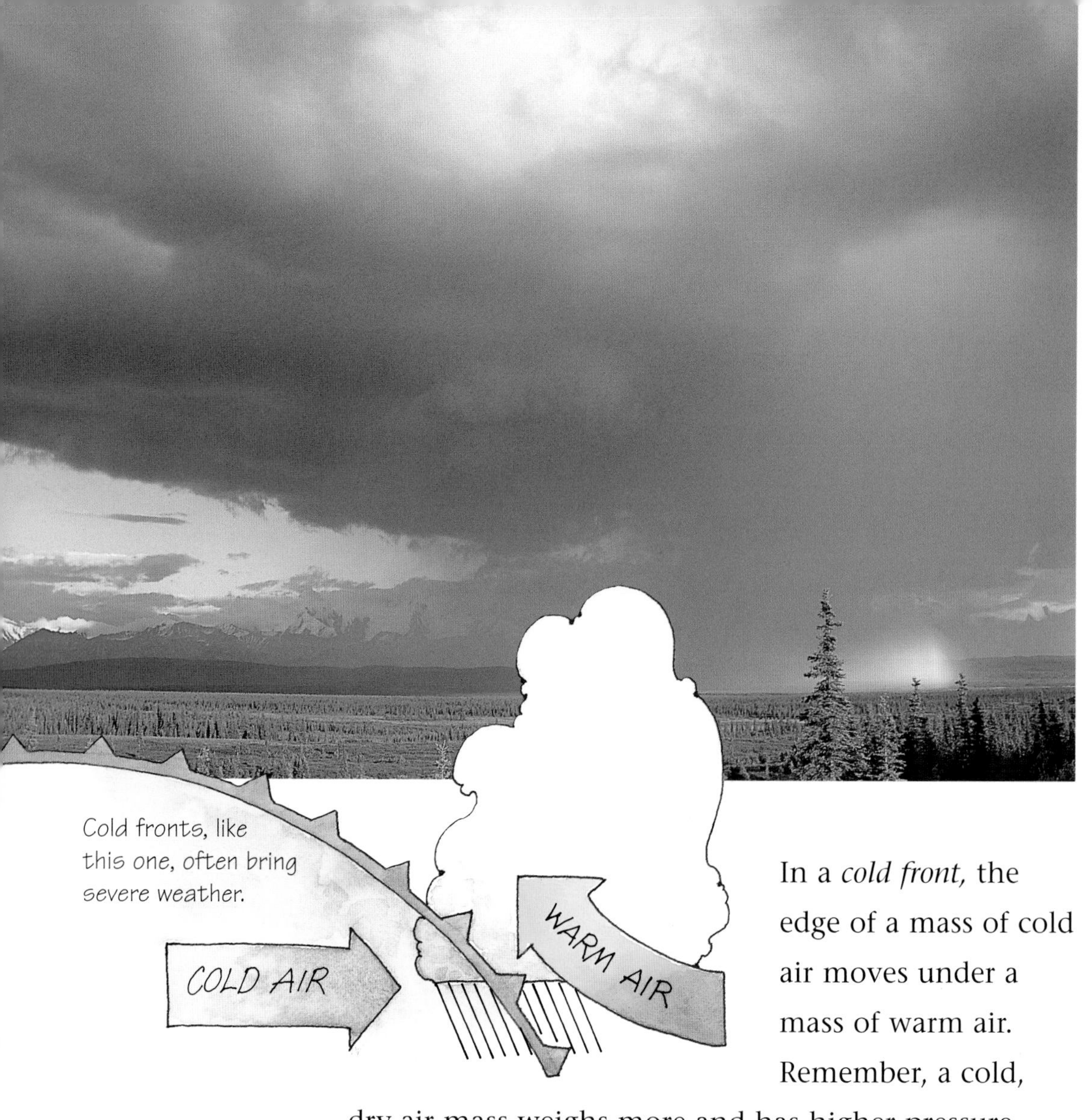

Cold fronts, like this one, often bring severe weather.

In a *cold front,* the edge of a mass of cold air moves under a mass of warm air. Remember, a cold, dry air mass weighs more and has higher pressure than a hot, wet one. If the two masses meet, the heavier cold air flows beneath the warm air, forcing the warm air to rise quickly. As the warm air rises, it cools. The water vapor in it may form rain or snow.

A *warm front* occurs when a warm air mass catches up with a cold air mass that is moving in the same direction. The warm air flows upward over the cold air, cooling as it rises. Its water vapor forms clouds that may travel hundreds of miles ahead of the front. These clouds slowly thicken, bringing rain, or maybe sleet or snow. And the wet weather may hang on for a while.

The weather around a cold front is usually more severe than the weather around a warm front. However, warm front weather will probably take longer to clear out. Do you see a front coming this way?

Warm fronts, like this one, usually take a while to clear.

How Warm and Cold Air Behave

Hmmmm . . . I wonder . . .
Is it true that warm air expands and rises?
How do I know that cold air really contracts and sinks?

GATHER TOOLS

- identical soda or juice bottles
- identical balloons
- bowls or pans
- hot water
- cold water
- ice cubes

Set up and give it a try

1 Place one balloon over each bottle's mouth.

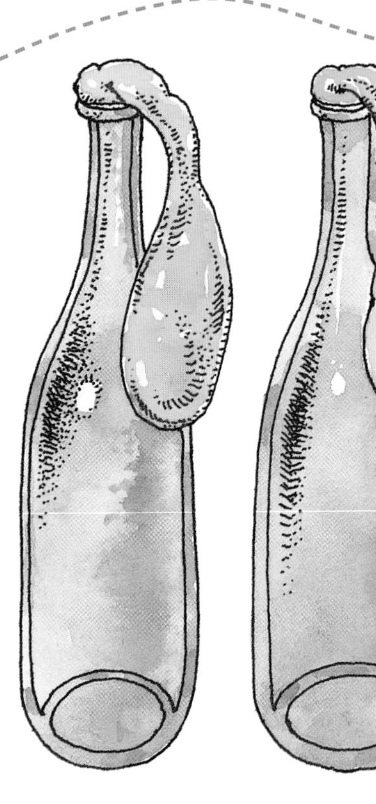

Set up a Control

Make another bottle and balloon setup, exactly like the other two, and put it in water that is room temperature.

2 In one bowl pour about 2 inches (5 cm) of hot water from the tap. In the other bowl pour ice water to the same depth.

3 Place one bottle in each bowl and watch what happens!

Try it again and again

- Redo the experiment without the bottles; blow up and tie the balloons and put them in water and ice.
- Try using water of different temperatures. Use a thermometer.

Now, write it down

Jot down what happened to each balloon and why you think it happened.

Compare your notes with the ones on page 32.

Tracking Violent Weather

Howdy, Partner! Some folks think of me as a modern cowgirl, er, cowperson. Instead of chasing bucking broncos on the range, I track bouncing twisters. Basically, I'm a meteorologist who's interested in tornadoes.

You may have noticed that I called the whirling storm a *twister.* Most of the time people use the word *tornado*. Both words mean the same thing, but I like the picture that the word *twister* conjures up. As a matter of fact, it looks like we have twister weather today—a great time for a storm chase and a good time for me to share some basic information about tornadoes.

First, you should know that we weather forecasters watch for violent weather around the clock. And we have some pretty fancy equipment to help us. For instance, weather satellites in space send us incredible photographs of the cloud tops. Weather balloons swirl in the upper atmosphere. They carry equipment that collects data such as temperature and air pressure. Radar stations on the ground pick up images of precipitation and storms.

***Precipitation** is any form of water that falls from clouds to the ground—rain, snow, sleet, or hail.*

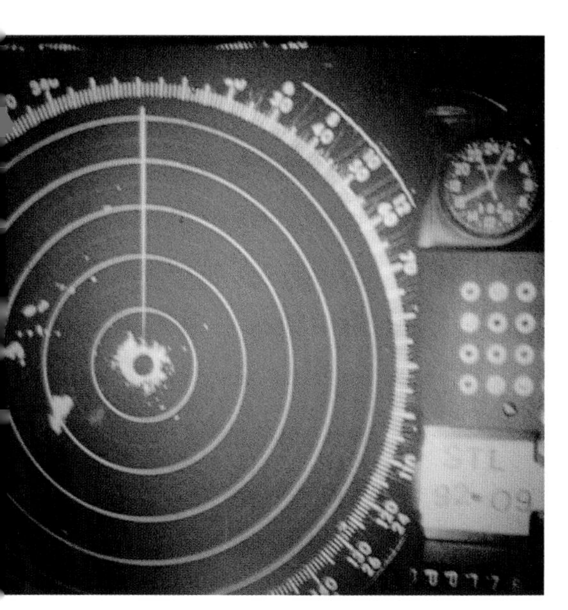

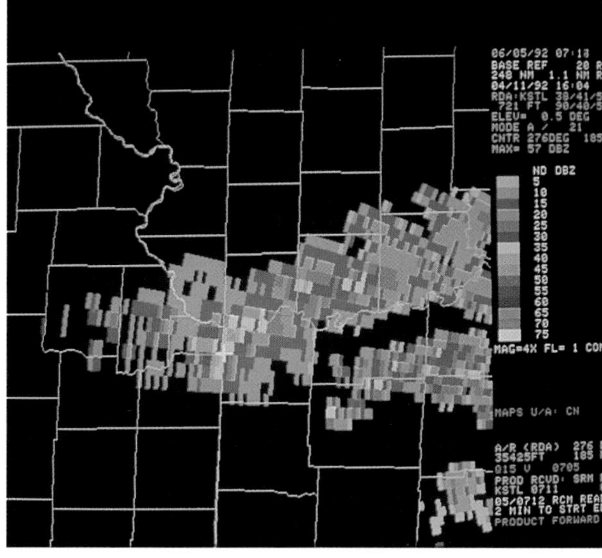

Perhaps the most exciting tool we have is *Doppler radar.* This special kind of radar works like the radar police use to catch speeders. It detects sudden changes in wind direction and speed. With Doppler radar we can see a tornado forming deep inside clouds and then warn people that severe weather is on the way.

Early radar equipment shows a storm's size and location (above left). But Doppler radar provides much more detail (above). The colors depict the speed and direction of winds, temperatures, and the types of precipitation. This storm produced golfball-sized hailstones!

Speaking of severe weather, look what's been brewing while we've been talking about tornadoes. That line of thunderstorms looks really mean! Our Doppler radar tells us that one of these is a supercell thunderstorm. A *supercell* is a towering storm that lives longer than others. It has an *updraft* (rising air) that rotates. Sounds like the start of a twister, doesn't it?

Tornadoes form in the same kind of air that cooks up thunderstorms. Usually, the air is hot and *humid* (moist), which makes it unstable. That means it's likely to rise rapidly. And if a cold front approaches, the heavier cold air flows under the warm air mass and pushes it up. Rising air may turn into a column of twisting air called a *funnel cloud.* If the air column grows stronger and stronger, it may become a tornado!

AHA!

Tornadoes are powerful storms that can do a lot of damage—yet most tornadoes last less than an hour and travel an average distance of about 20 miles (36 km).

Up ahead is a wall cloud. A *wall cloud* is a dark, rounded cloud at the base of a thunderstorm. No rain falls from it because the rising wind is too strong. A funnel could drop down at any time. If it does, then we have a tornado.

Not all funnel clouds "touch down," or drop to the ground. But when they do, they can do a lot of damage. Meteorologists measure a tornado's strength by the damage it leaves behind. We use the Fujita scale to rate tornadoes from F0 (the weakest) to F5 (the strongest).

Those of us who have been close to a twister can tell you that they are frightening. The updrafts near the funnel can pick up cars and trucks. The whirling dust is so thick that it's hard to see what's going on. Hail often falls, and sometimes the hailstones are as big as eggs!

Why is a tornado's strength measured by the damage it leaves behind? That is largely because it's difficult to predict where the middle of the storm will be, and it's dangerous to get equipment there.

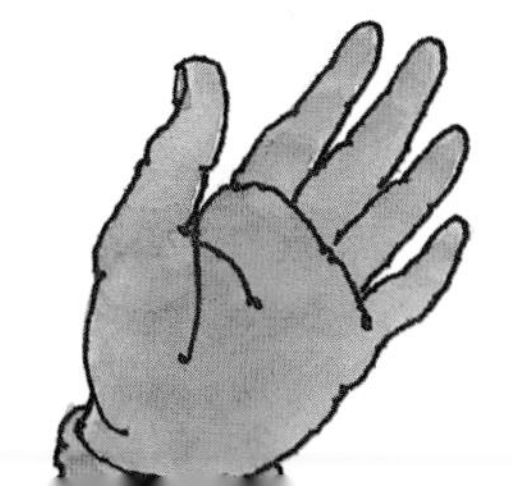

Tornadoes are the most powerful storms on Earth. That's why it's important to watch out for them. They can pack winds of more than 200 miles per hour (320 kph). Most tornadoes are skinny, several hundred yards or meters in diameter. But some monsters get to be 1 1/2 miles (2.4 km) wide.

Take my advice. Don't run after tornadoes—or any other violent storms. Storm chasing is a job for professionals who understand the risks involved in studying violent weather. We hope we learn enough to keep everyone safe from twisters.

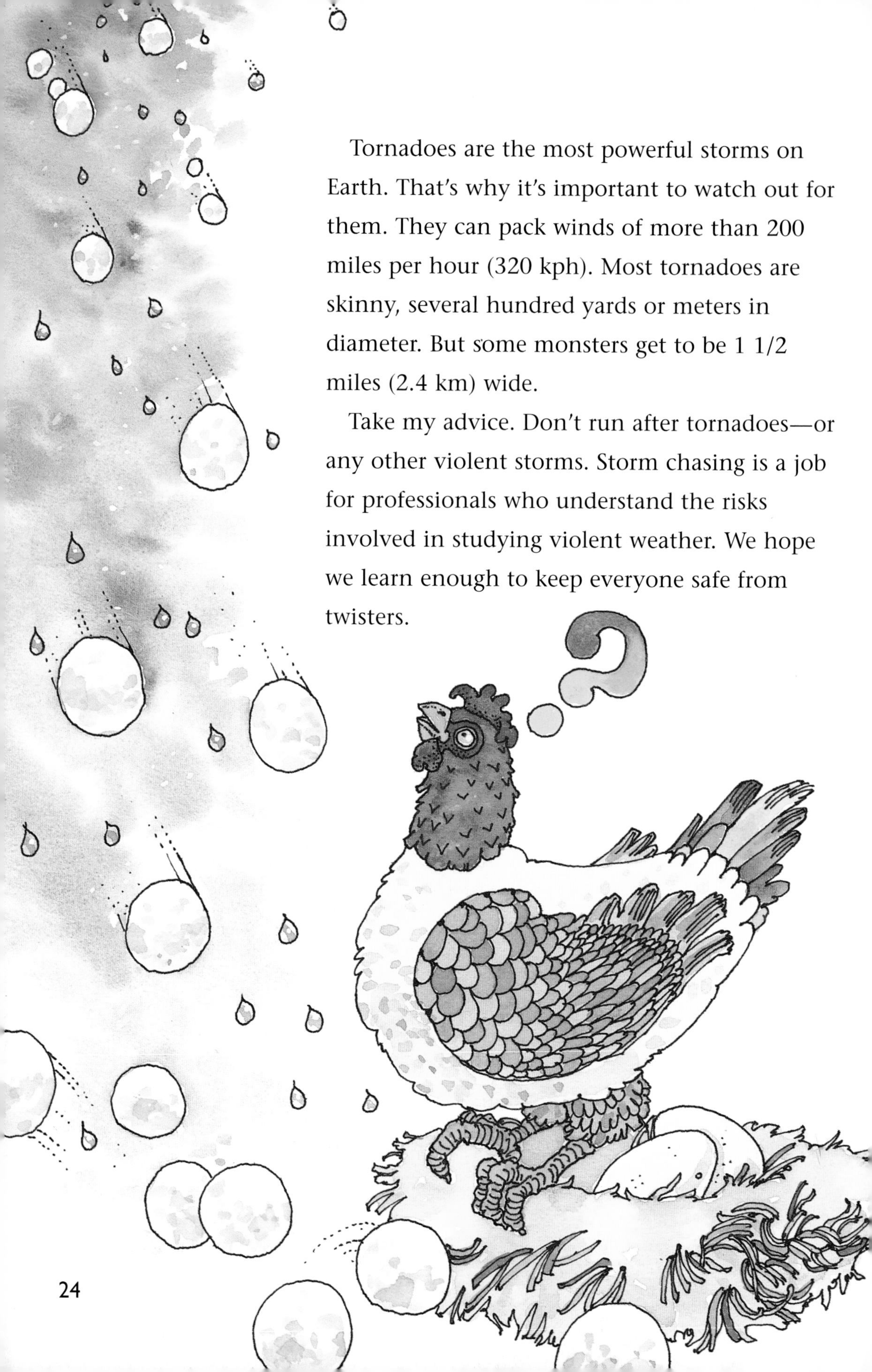

Do you know where tornadoes are most likely to strike? The central United States encounters more tornadoes than any other place on Earth. Oklahoma is in the middle of Tornado Alley, an area of the United States that has frequent twisters. Other countries have twisters, too, but not as often. In fact, Bangladesh, a nation in south-central Asia, had a devastating tornado in 1996.

Looks like our storm is breaking up. That's no surprise. There aren't tornadoes in every storm. In fact, we storm chasers do a lot of driving and study lots of weather data. I usually see only two or three tornadoes in a year.

When a twisting funnel cloud drops down, look out! You have a tornado!

Weather Bulletins from the Past

I'm Sherlock Storms, climate detective—or *climatologist,* if you want to get technical. It's my job to figure out what the weather was like on Earth hundreds, thousands, even millions of years ago. Actually, it's not as difficult as it sounds. There are plenty of clues.

Finding out what the weather was like a few hundred years ago is fairly easy. Old weather diaries and almanacs offer terrific data. Believe me, people have always loved the topic of weather.

It's harder to find written weather records if I want to go back a thousand years or more. That's when I might go to California to check out the giant sequoias. These trees are among the oldest and largest living things on Earth. They can live for up to 3,000 years.

Rings across the trunk of a giant sequoia reveal what the weather was like for every year

of the tree's life. A wide ring means that the weather was warm or moist and the tree grew well that year. A narrow ring means that the weather was cold or dry, so the tree grew little.

This is a page from a weather journal that was kept more than 200 years ago!

Another way to find out about Earth's climate of the last few thousand years is by digging in Europe's peat bogs. *Peat* is a mass of brownish, decayed plants like moss. In some places, peat collects in bogs that are thousands of feet deep. Peat preserves plant pollen. Suppose I dig 100 feet (30 m) into a peat bog. From certain clues, I know that this layer is about 6,000 years old. As I examine it, I find lots of pollen from shrubs and trees that grow in wet, rainy climates. I can conclude that the climate here was wet 6,000 years ago.

But how do we learn about the weather on Earth millions of years ago? Fossils tell us a lot. These remains of plants and animals are found in layers of rock. A fossil reveals something about the weather during the time it was living.

AHA!

Scientists don't have to cut down or kill a tree to examine its annual growth rings. Scientists use an *increment borer*—a long, thin metal tube—to *bore* (drill) a hole in the tree trunk, and then they take out a core sample of the rings.

I don't do all the dirty detective work. This person in Greenland is cutting ice samples.

For example, fossils of palms and ferns tell us the climate was hot and steamy. Fossils of sea animals tell us an ancient sea once covered the area.

Some scientists have even gone to Antarctica (brrr!) to investigate Earth's past. The ice there is very thick—up to 15,700 feet deep (4,800 m). And deep down, it is very ancient. The scientists drill deep holes to find ice that formed millions of years ago. Air trapped in this ancient ice reveals what Earth's atmosphere was like then. For example, scientists found ancient air that contained much less carbon dioxide than air does today.

When I put all these clues together, a fairly clear picture of Earth's past weather comes into focus. For most of the past 500 million years, Earth's weather has been warm and mild. But the fine-weather times, or *interglacial* (IHN tuhr GLAY shuhl) periods, were interrupted by ice ages, called *glacial* (GLAY shuhl) periods. In glacial periods, thousands of feet of ice covered much of the land.

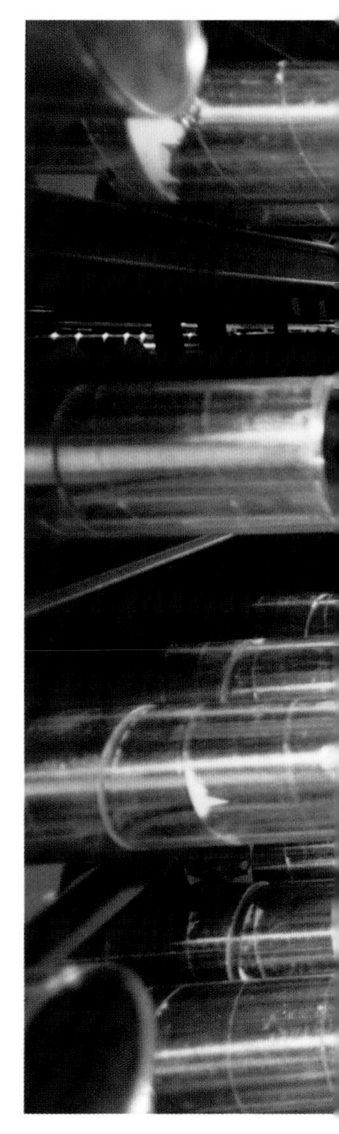

Workers at the National Core Laboratory in Boulder, Colorado, store ice for further testing. Even a snowball would keep in this room!

Of course, we don't live in a glacial period now. But it's important to study the slow changes in Earth's weather. These patterns can reveal future conditions. Will we have another glacial period someday? Will the greenhouse effect warm the earth up? All I can say is: "Stay tuned."

Weather Folklore

Good morning! I hope you're not planning to go sailing. Just look at that red sky. It reminds me of the old saying: "Red sky at night, sailors' delight. Red sky in morning, sailors take warning." You say you never heard that before? Well, I collect weather proverbs. *Proverbs* are sayings that generations pass down by word of mouth. Some proverbs are based on scientific ideas, but others, like this one, are not. Yet people still like to quote them. Let me share some more with you.

"Hen scratches and filly tails:
Get ready to lower your topsails."

Scientific basis? Yes. "Hen scratches" and "filly tails" are folk terms for cirrus clouds. *Cirrus* are very high clouds made of ice crystals. They travel fast and usually warn of rain approaching within 24 hours. Sailors watch for these clouds.

"Year of snow,
Crops will grow."

Scientific basis? Yes. A heavy snowfall protects plant roots in the ground from frigid air. Also, snow that stays on the ground in spring keeps tender blossoms from opening too early.

"A bad winter is betide (will happen)
If hair grows thick on a bear's hide."

Scientific basis? No. Animals grow heavy coats when they have lots to eat in summer. Growth of fur has nothing to do with the coming winter.

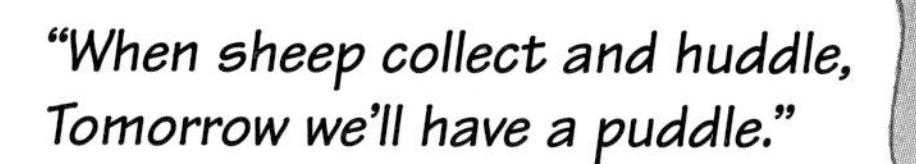

"When sheep collect and huddle,
Tomorrow we'll have a puddle."

Scientific basis? Yes. Animals sense the changing weather and become nervous. They huddle together for comfort.

"Seaweed dry, sunny sky;
Seaweed wet, rain you'll get."

Scientific basis? Yes. A piece of dried seaweed hanging on your porch absorbs moisture from the air. If it turns wet, the air is full of water vapor. Rain may be near.

"If bees to distance wing their flight,
Days are warm and skies are bright.
But when their flight ends near
their home,
Stormy weather's sure to come."

Scientific basis? Yes. When humidity increases before a rainstorm, bees return to the hive for shelter. In fact, bees usually produce less honey during very cloudy, rainy summers.

"If the crescent moon lies on her back,
She sucks the wet into her lap."

Scientific basis? No. The proverb suggests that no rain will fall when the crescent moon looks like an upright cup, because the moon won't spill water. This idea has no basis in science.

Time To Think

"The time has come," the Walrus said,
"To talk of many things:
Of shoes—and ships—and sealing wax—
Of cabbages—and kings—
And why the sea is boiling hot—
And whether pigs have wings. . . ."

From *Through the Looking-Glass*
by Lewis Carroll

Lab Notes

Here are some notes and findings you may have made when doing the labs presented in this book. There aren't any right or wrong notes. In fact, you probably made many observations different from the ones given here. That's okay. What can you conclude from them? If a lab didn't turn out the way you thought it would, that's okay too. Do you know why it didn't? If not, go back and find out. After doing a lab, did you come up with more questions, different from the ones you had when you started? If you did, good. Grab your journal and your science kit and start looking for more answers!

pages 12-13 *Make and Use a Barometer*

When the air pressure is high, the air pushes the balloon down, and the needle moves up. When the air pressure drops, the balloon rises, and the needle moves down. To get the most precise measurements, it helps to put the jars on a stiff board to keep them level.

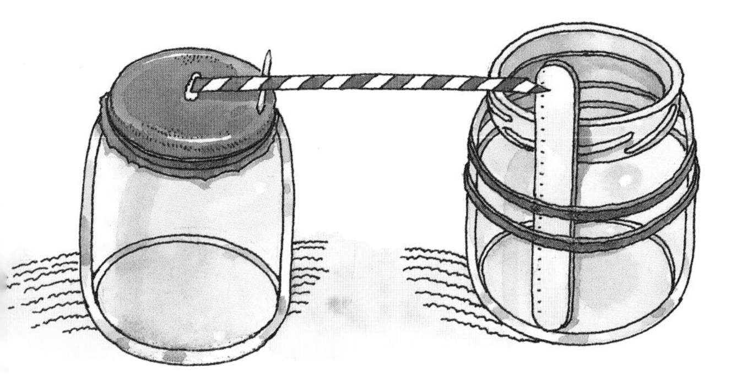

pages 18-19 *How Warm and Cold Air Behave*

The balloon on the bottle that sits in hot water expands. Nothing is added to the balloon or to the jar, so a person could conclude that the air inside takes up more space when it is heated. In ice water, the balloon contracts and sinks because the cooled air inside the bottle takes up less space. The balloon in the control experiment does not expand or contract, which helps confirm that the change in temperature makes the air—and thus the balloons—take up more or less space.